FRANK RODGERS

Bumps in
the Night

Illustrated by Philip Hopman

Hippo

Scholastic Children's Books
Commonwealth House, 1-19 New Oxford Street,
London WC1A 1NU, UK
a division of Scholastic Ltd
London ~ New York ~ Toronto ~ Sydney ~ Auckland

Published in the UK by Scholastic Ltd, 1996

Text copyright © Frank Rodgers, 1996
Illustrations copyright © Philip Hopman, 1996

ISBN 0 590 13714 X

Typeset by Backup   Design and Production, London
Printed by Cox & Wyman Ltd, Reading, Berks

10 9 8 7 6

Chapter 1

Sam and Katie Pickle were excited.

Their mum and dad had bought a little café in a country village and the family were going to live in the flat above it. The café was called The Hungry Horse and the Pickles were thrilled to bits with it.

"It looks so cosy and welcoming,"

smiled Mr Pickle.

"It's going to be the best café in the world," replied Mrs Pickle, and Sam and Katie agreed.

On the day of their arrival they went to buy food at the village store. It was then that people began to talk.

"You've bought The Hungry Horse Café?" gasped Mrs Kettle in surprise, her hairy eyebrows doing a little dance. "But it's haunted, you know."

"Yes, indeed," agreed Mr Faucett, the greengrocer, "by a thing that goes bump in the night."

"And what a noise it makes too!" cried little Miss Mantle. "*Bump ... ooooh! Bump ... ooooh!*"

"Very scary," they all said.
"Oh, dear," said Mr Pickle.

"Not only that," Miss Mantle went on, her little eyes jumping up and down like ping-pong balls, "but it's probably the ghost of a rascally robber or a horrible hairy highwayman. So many things have gone missing in the village over the years, you see."

"They certainly have," Mrs Chimmly chimed in. "That café of yours should be called The Greedy Ghost!"

"What sort of things have gone missing?" asked Mrs Pickle.

"My silver watch and chain," said Mr Faucett.

"My gold ring," said Mrs Kettle.

"My brass thimble," said Mrs Chimmly.

"My little cut-glass perfume bottle," said Miss Mantle.

"Lots of other things too," said Mr Faucett. "And we're sure that the ghost is responsible."

"Oh, dear," said Mr Pickle.

Chapter 2

That night, as she and Sam settled down to sleep in the little flat above the café, Katie said, "Do you really think there is a ghost, Mum?"

Mrs Pickle laughed. "I wouldn't think so, Katie," she said. "People sometimes let their imaginations run away with them. I don't think it's a ghost who is stealing those things from the people in the village, do you?"

Katie shook her head slowly. "No..." she replied.

Then Sam piped up. "But what causes the bumps in the night, Mum?"

"Oh, the bumps in the night are probably caused by the old plumbing, Sam. Air in the pipes makes them bang," she said.

"Or it could be the timbers of the house creaking and groaning like old bones," said his dad. "This is an old building. Old buildings complain, you know."

They kissed Sam and Katie goodnight and went to bed themselves.

"Bumps in the night," scoffed Katie when they were left alone. *"Bump ... ooooh ... bump ... ooooh...* Of course it's just the plumbing!"

"Yes," agreed Sam. "Just the old house complaining."

"Or," giggled Katie, "it could be an elephant clog-dancing on the roof. *Bump ... ta-raaa! Bump ... ta-raaa!"*

Sam laughed and joined in the fun. "Or a gorilla on a pogo stick. *Bump ... wheee! Bump ... wheee!*"

They were both laughing now.

"It could be a pirate with a wooden leg!" cried Katie. "*Bump ... ooo-aar! Bump ... ooo-aar!*"

Their bubbling laughter rang round the room. It filled up their ears so much that at first they didn't hear the noises.

Then Katie suddenly said, "Shhh!
Listen, Sam!"

Sam stopped laughing and listened.

Faintly, from above their heads in
the attic, came some unmistakable
sounds.

Bump ... ooooh! Bump ... ooooh!

"Oh!" gasped Sam. "Katie … you don't think…?"

Bump … ooooh! went the noises, a little louder this time.

"It's just the plumbing!" squeaked Katie.

Bump … ooooh…!

"Or the old timbers!" squealed Sam, jumping on to his sister's bed.

BUMP ... OOOH!

"Aaah!" they gasped. "It's the ghost! The house is haunted after all!" And they rushed out of their bedroom and into Mum and Dad's.

The Pickles huddled together on the big bed and listened.

BUMP ... OOOOH! BUMP ... OOOOH!

"Er … it's just the plumbing," said Mr Pickle.

"Or the old timbers…" said Mrs Pickle.

BUMP … OOOOH … OOOOH!

"Are you sure?" asked Sam and Katie.

"Well … perhaps it would be a good idea if we made up beds for you in our room for tonight," said Mum and Dad.

Chapter 3

Next morning in the bright sunshine the little flat above the café didn't seem scary at all.

"We were very silly yesterday," said Mr Pickle. "Imagine being scared of a few bumps in the night."

"Why don't we look around?" suggested Mrs Pickle. "We might find out what's causing the noises."

"Yes!" cried Sam and Katie. "Let's explore!"

So they searched every nook and cranny, poking their noses into corners and cupboards. Mr Pickle checked the piping and tapped on the walls. He even looked up the chimney.

But nowhere did they find anything that might have made the *bump ... oooh!* noises.

"What about the attic?" said Katie.

"Oh, dear, I'd forgotten all about that," said Mr Pickle.

He got the ladder out and propped it up against the hatch.

Up he went.

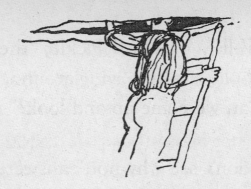

Creeeak... The wooden hatch groaned as Mr Pickle pushed it open. The rest of the family gazed up at him and held their breath.

"What do you see?" asked Mrs Pickle.

"Well …" said Mr Pickle, "there's a lot of old furniture lying around."

"Can we come up and look?" asked Sam.

"I don't see why not," answered his dad. "It seems perfectly safe."

One by one they climbed the ladder and went into the attic.

It was like the inside of a junk shop.
Chairs and tables, trunks and boxes,
drawers and cupboards lying higgledy-
piggledy. There was even an old
rocking-horse.

"It's wonderful!" cried Sam.

"Like Aladdin's Cave!" exclaimed
Katie.

Mr Pickle pointed to a hole in the roof. "Look," he said, "that could explain all the noises. The wind could whistle through that gap…"

"Going *ooooh*…" smiled Mrs Pickle.

"Yes," grinned Mr Pickle, "and it could move the rocking-horse, making it go *bump*!"

"So there you are," said Mrs Pickle smugly. "It's all explained. There is no ghost."

Katie leaned close to Sam and whispered, "I was hoping we really had a ghost, Sam."

Sam nodded and whispered back, "Me too. It would've been fun."

The Pickles then began to explore the attic and Katie opened a little trunk and looked inside.

"Oh, look everyone!" she said. "Old photographs."

She picked them up and handed them round.

"Here's one of The Hungry Horse Café," said Mr Pickle.

Mrs Pickle looked at the faded black and white photograph and said, "My goodness, this must have been taken a long, long time ago."

"Who's that old man standing in front of the café?" asked Sam.

His mum turned the photograph over and saw there was some faint writing on the back.

"As far as I can make out it says *T. Greenberry. Proprietor*," she said. "He must have been the original owner."

"This photograph would look lovely hanging in our café," said Mr Pickle. "It would be a nice link with the past."

Katie looked at the old man again. "He looks nice," she said.

Sam nodded in agreement. "Smiley," he said. "As if he really loved living here."

"Maybe he still does," Katie whispered to Sam, taking him aside.

"You mean…" Sam began.

"Yes," whispered Katie, her eyes sparkling. "I think we've found our ghost!"

Chapter 4

That night, Katie and Sam lay awake, waiting.

The minutes ticked by towards midnight and they became sleepier and sleepier.

"Perhaps there isn't a ghost after all," murmured Sam.

Katie yawned and snuggled down,

sighing. "Perhaps you're right," she said.

Bump ... ooooh!

Katie and Sam sat bolt upright in their beds. "What was that?" they cried.

Bump ... ooooh! went the noise again.

Their bedroom door opened and in came Mum and Dad.

"It's the ghost!" chorused Katie and Sam.

Mr Pickle shook his head. "It's just the wind blowing through that hole in the roof," he said. "Go back to sleep."

But Katie and Sam got out of bed.

"I think we should go and look," said Katie.

Mum glanced at Dad and they both shrugged.

"Why not?" said Mrs Pickle. "Let's find out once and for all."

Bump ... ooooh!

Everyone looked up.

"The noise is definitely coming from the attic," said Mr Pickle. "Let's investigate."

Once more he put the ladder up against the hatch. "Er ... it'll probably be dark up there," he said, unsure.

"Perhaps I should fetch a torch?"

"We don't have one, dear," said Mrs Pickle, and before Mr Pickle could protest, she began to climb the ladder. Stealthily she crept upwards.

Creeeaak… The hatch opened and she disappeared into the attic.

A few seconds later Mrs Pickle poked her head down through the opening and whispered, "Come on up."

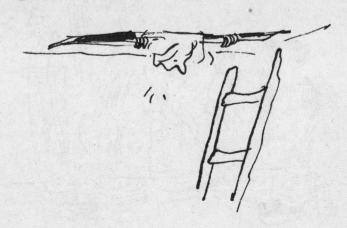

One by one they followed her until all four were standing together among the shadowy bits of furniture. The moonlight shone in through the small window and the hole in the roof, and the light in the hall shone up from below so the attic wasn't as dark as Mr Pickle had feared.

Sam looked at the rocking-horse and gasped. "Oh!" he cried. "Look … it's moving!"

Mr Pickle smiled. "Ah," he said, "just as I thought. The wind has blown in through the hole and—"

Bump`... OOOOH!

Everyone jumped.

The noise had come from behind them!

Startled, everyone whirled round and saw...

The ghost!

It was the kindly old man from the photograph.

"I knew it!" Katie whispered in glee and Sam grinned from ear to ear.

The old man didn't seem to have noticed them. He stood beside a small table rubbing his shin and shaking his head. "Can't see a thing without my glasses," he muttered. "Keep on bumping into things."

Mr and Mrs Pickle gaped at him in astonishment.

"Oh, dear," murmured Mr Pickle. "I was wrong. We *do* have a ghost."

"This house is haunted after all," gasped Mrs Pickle.

"Hooray!" yelled Sam and Katie.

"What ... who?" The ghost looked up sharply and bumped his head on a brass lampshade. *Bump!* "Ooooh!" he cried.

He rubbed his head and stared at the family. "Who are you?" he asked.

"Er ... we're the Pickle family," replied Mr Pickle. "We live here now."

"Ah," said the ghost, "of course ... the new owners." He bowed.

"Delighted to meet you. My name is Tobias Greenberry. I built this place, you know, and lived here up to my death a hundred years ago." He smiled. "I liked it so much I couldn't bear to leave it. That's why I'm still here."

"You're the thing that goes bump in the night!" cried Katie.

Tobias nodded ruefully and rubbed his head and then his shin. "I've lost my glasses, you see. Can't see properly without them. Keep on bumping into things."

"And going *ooooh*!" said Sam with a grin.

Tobias nodded again. "Sorry if I disturbed you," he said. "It's just that some ghosts are more solid than others. That's why I bump into things rather than go *through* them." He rubbed his shin again. "You haven't come across a pair of glasses, have you?"

The Pickles shook their heads.

"I'm afraid not," said Mr Pickle.

The old man sighed. "Looks like I'll just have to blunder around going *bump ... ooooh* until I find them," he said.

"Perhaps someone took them," suggested Katie.

"Yes," said Sam, "the same person who took the things from the people in the village."

"Oh," said Tobias. "You mean other things have gone missing as well?"

Mrs Pickle nodded. "The people in the village think that you're to blame, Tobias. They said that the café should be called The Greedy Ghost."

Tobias was shocked. "What?" he cried. "But that's terrible! I've never stolen anything in my life. How can people think that of me? I must clear my name ... but how?"

As the family pondered on this the moon came out from behind a cloud and bathed everything in a silvery glow.

Suddenly something caught Sam's eye.

"Look," he said, stepping forward and picking up a large black feather and two small grey ones. "Where did these come from?"

Mr Pickle examined them and nodded his head.

"Aha!" he said with a grin. "I think we may have found our robber!"

Mrs Pickle looked at the feathers and smiled too. "These are a jackdaw's feathers," she said.

"Yes … they like to take things, don't they?" said Katie.

"Bright, shiny things," said Sam.

"Like thimbles, rings, watches…" said Mr Pickle.

"And glasses!" cried Tobias. He clapped his hands. "Come to think of it, I have seen a jackdaw coming and going through that hole in the roof. Do you really think that it could be to blame for all the missing things?"

"It certainly could," said Mr Pickle. "And we're going to find out, Tobias … tomorrow!"

Chapter 5

After breakfast next morning the Pickle family went into the back garden. Tobias's pale face peered at them from the attic window, watching anxiously.

There were quite a few trees in the garden and also quite a few birds flying about. Amid the whistling and trilling of the birds the Pickles heard loud, harsh, *tchack … tchack* sounds.

"That," said Mr Pickle, "is our friend the jackdaw."

They heard them again and Katie pointed. "There!" she cried.

Everyone looked up into the huge chestnut tree at the bottom of the garden. Just visible near the top was the dark shape of a large nest. Out of it flew a black bird with a grey band round the lower part of its head.

"That's the jackdaw, all right," exclaimed Mr Pickle.

He went into the outhouse and returned with a long ladder which he propped against the tree.

"Be careful, dear," called Mrs Pickle as he began to climb.

"I will," replied Mr Pickle, as he went higher and higher.

The jackdaw was annoyed at the intrusion and flapped around the tree, croaking loudly like a stick rattling against a fence.

A few seconds later, Mr Pickle disappeared from sight into the foliage of the tree. The family waited anxiously below for him to reappear again.

Tobias hadn't moved from the window in the attic.

Minutes passed and Mr Pickle didn't appear.

"Oh, dear," said Mrs Pickle. "I do hope he's all right."

Just then Mr Pickle's legs came into view as he climbed back down the ladder.

"Hooray!" shouted Sam and Katie. "Dad's okay!"

In the attic Tobias jumped for joy and bumped his head against the brass lamp again.

Bump! "Ooooh!"

Mr Pickle descended slowly towards his wife and children. When he reached the ground they saw that he was smiling happily.

"It was like a blooming treasure trove up there!" he said, laughing.

"That jackdaw's nest was stuffed with all sorts of bright things." He reached into the big pockets of his jacket and brought out things which glittered in the sunlight.

A brass thimble ... a silver watch and chain ... a cut-glass perfume bottle ... a gold ring ... a diamond brooch ... a silver spoon ... and finally, a pair of glasses.

He held the things up one by one to show Tobias. The pale, ghostly face at the window peered hard, then broke into a huge grin. It disappeared from view as Tobias jumped for joy again.

Down from the attic drifted the familiar *bump ... ooooh!*

The family laughed.

"Poor Tobias," said Mrs Pickle. "But I'm sure that's the last time he'll bump into anything now he's got his glasses back."

"And he'll be delighted that his name is cleared at last," said Mr Pickle. "We must give these things back and tell everyone who the *real* robber was!"

Chapter 6

Tobias was thrilled to bits. He danced round and round the attic laughing and singing happily. And because he was wearing his glasses he didn't bump into one thing.

"It'll be nice and quiet up here from now on, won't it, Tobias," grinned Mr Pickle.

"It certainly will," replied Tobias. "because now that I've found my glasses I can wander about all over the house."

"Oh…" said Mr Pickle. "*All* over the house, Tobias? Including the café?"

"Especially the café!" replied Tobias
cheerfully. "Oh, it'll be so nice to go
back to my old haunts again!"

"But ..." stammered Mr Pickle,
"won't you frighten away our
customers?"

"Oh, don't worry about that," smiled Tobias. "I'll stay in the kitchen until they get used to me. I used to be a great cook, you know. In fact," he added happily, "since I've become a ghost I've learnt some terrific new recipes!"

"Fantastic!" cried Sam and Katie. "We'll have a spook for a cook!"

Everyone roared with laughter.

And that is why The Hungry Horse Café was renamed The Spooky Cook Café and became famous throughout the countryside for some rather strange dishes on its menu…

Ghosted Cheese…

Spook-etti…

I-Scream…

And a yummy cake covered in black icing, silver stars and big lumps of dark chocolate called *Bumps In The Night*.

The End

Bumps in
the Night

"Perhaps there isn't a ghost after all," murmured Sam.

Katie yawned and snuggled down, sighing. "Perhaps you're right," she said.

Bump ... ooooh!

Katie and Sam sat bolt upright in their beds. "What was that?" they cried.

Bump ... ooooh! went the noise again.

Their bedroom door opened and in came Mum and Dad.

"It's the ghost!" chorused Katie and Sam.

Dare you try *another* Young Hippo Spooky?

Ghost Dog
Eleanor Allen

The Screaming Demon Ghostie
Jean Chapman

The Green Hand
Tessa Krailing

Smoke Cat
Linda Newbery

The Kings' Castle
Ann Ruffell

Scarem's House
Malcolm Yorke

These Young Hippo Magic stories are fantastic!

My Friend's a Gris-Quok!
Malorie Blackman

Diggory and the Boa Conductor
The Little Pet Dragon
Philippa Gregory

Broomstick Services
Ann Jungman

The Marmalade Pony
Linda Newbery

Mr Wellington Boots
Ann Ruffell

The Wishing Horse
Malcolm Yorke